JESUS
OUTSIDE
THE BOX

'Twelve Spiritual Tales of the Unexpected'

JESUS OUTSIDE THE BOX

'Twelve Spiritual Tales of the Unexpected'

Mark Townsend

Illustrated by James Townsend

Foreword by Richard Rohr OFM

BOOKS

Winchester, UK
Washington, USA

First published by O-Books, 2008
Reprinted 2010
O Books is an imprint of John Hunt Publishing Ltd., The Bothy, Deershot Lodge, Park Lane, Ropley,
Hants, SO24 0BE, UK
office1@o-books.net
www.o-books.com

For distributor details and how to order please visit the 'Ordering' section on our website.

Text copyright Mark Townsend 2010

ISBN: 978 1 84694 326 3

A CIP catalogue record for this book is available from the British Library.

Design: Stuart Davies

Printed and bound by CPI Group (UK) Ltd, Croydon, CR0 4YY

We operate a distinctive and ethical publishing philosophy in all
areas of its business, from its global network of authors to
production and worldwide distribution.

CONTENTS

Dedicated to, and in loving memory of,
Margaret Wickstead (1923-2008)

A founding member of the Movement for the
Ordination of Women, and one of the most beloved
and respected servants of Hereford Diocese.

Dear Margaret,
You were always so passionate for change, and
fought tirelessly for the constant reformation of
outdated structures and demoralizing religiosity.

Your enthusiasm was infectious, your optimism was
unstoppable and your inspiration will last forever.

You were a fearless defender of those who saw the spark
of God in places where others dared not venture. Your
love for the grace-filled one shone out and brightened
the many radical clergy you so generously gave your
time to. As one of them, I will ever look back on
our friendship as the greatest of blessings.

You were so good to me and me family - the most
loyal, solid and constant supporter, even after the
mess and muddle I ended up in.
You never gave up on me. I miss you so much
and will never forget you.

Thank you from the bottom of my heart.

May you Rest in Peace!

You are unique, you are beautiful, you were made in Heaven, there is no-one like you, you are special, you are once only, you are never to be repeated, you are incredible, you are a child of heaven!

ACKNOWLEDGMENTS

Affection and appreciation go to my two little angels, Aisha and Jamie, for being the best two kiddies a father could ask for. Aisha is a wonderful writer as you'll see when you come to her poetic and wise words in the final Tale. Jamie is a true Magi in the making.

My brother James! Gosh what a creative guy he is. Put a camera in his hands and he becomes an artist par excellence. All the photography found within these pages is his for which I am profoundly grateful.

I am also indebted to two very special Priests of the Catholic Church; my spiritual Mentor, Fr. Richard Rohr, who honoured me by writing the wonderful Foreword, and my best man, Fr. Gerry Proctor, who gave me such a great gift when he agreed to write the Introduction. Both these men have summed up quite beautifully where me and my book are coming from.

Thanks also go to my fantastic colleague in the magical arts, Dave Taylor, my invaluable spiritual sounding board, Rev. Caroline George, and the wonderfully creative Judy Dinen for the beautiful poem that heads the first Tale.

Finally thanks to all who have walked beside me at various points in my life and are thus essential characters in the living Tale of my life…

Note: This book is a work of fiction. Though based on biblical accounts these stories are from the author's imagination and are not to be taken literally or seen as 'commentaries on a text'. The ideas contained are designed to prompt the reader's own imagination rather than describe actual religious beliefs or notions about deity.

Since the last edition of this book I've made many new friends, some of whom have been a tremendous support and influence on my more recent travels. There are far too many to mention them all personally.

However, I would like to say a huge thank you all those I've had the privilege of getting to know through the world of earth-

based spirituality and in particularly the Druidic community, especially Philip and Stephanie Carr-Gomm who've been a constant support. I also wish to thank the many I've encountered through my connections with the Progressive Christian Network, in particular the current Chair, Rev. John Churcher. Without the PCN and other Progressive and Liberal Christian groups I may have given up on the dear old Church for good. Finally I must also thank The Rev. Peter Owen Jones for his personal support and for his incredibly infectious outside the box ethos. Through his television documentaries he has given us all a taste of what the spiritual quest can be like, if we are only prepared to live a little more at the edges and boundaries of things.

FOREWORD

Stories leave room for the soul to grow inside of them. Stories leave space for silence and awakening instead of just giving you answers. Stories speak to head, heart, and spiritual imagination instead of merely to the intellect. It is no surprise that most great spiritual teachers were also story tellers in some form: Jesus, Buddha, Teresa of Avila, most Zen masters, Anthony de Mello, and even the Exodus stories which were attributed to Moses, or the Genesis stories which formed our Western psyche.

Once we became convinced that people needed clear conclusions instead of spiritual process, religion stopped telling stories and preferred systematic theology instead. Henceforward, our concerns became consistency more than conversion, predictability more than changed lives; order itself more than the God created world of constant disorder. It was such a world that Jesus accepted and even loved. It is that world of "disorder" that Mark Townsend brings to life and wonderment in this book.

When religion stopped telling stories, it quickly degenerated into fundamentalism, where there was only one level of meaning to everything, and ironically that level was the most watered down of all. Spiritual imagination lost out in favor of prescribed belief systems and tight belonging systems. Spiritual curiosity, the preferred vantage point of the saints, has been in rather constant decline ever since. We did not need to search, seek, and discover our deepest level of desire. We settled for religious formula and sacramental technique.

We did not need the Holy Spirit to "teach us all things" and "remind us of all things" and "renew all things". We already have our answers for everything. One does not need spiritual curiosity, Jesus called it "knocking" and "seeking", when you already have all of your conclusions in place. Although religion is clearly about the journey toward divine union, we seemed to prefer divine order instead. I guess it gives us a sense of control. Union never does.

But you are about to be made curious! You are about to be enchanted. You are about to say "Why didn't I ever think of it that way?" You are about to be invited to "spiritually think", and I think that is the true and deepest meaning of contemplation. You are about to be invited into divine union, ironically by struggling with the disorder, the humor, the inconsistency, the freedom that God has to break God's own rules. The word for that is mercy. The word for that is forgiveness. The word for that is grace. You will "feel" it, and know it, in this book.

As we call forth more writers and "magicians" like Fr. Mark Townsend, we might just discover a whole new meaning to priesthood. If priests are those who "mediate" between the human and the divine, if priests are agents of transformation, if priests are those who fashion new images so the soul can see rightly, then this is indeed a very priestly book. We cannot just do such priestly work at the altar, with official sacraments, but we must be helped to sacramentalize every level of our lives. You have a good helper here.

Ironically, some novelists, playwrights, and poets are doing it better than some of us who stand at the altar. All I know, is that whoever creates such holy connections is priest and prophet for me.

Fr. Richard Rohr, O.F.M.
Center for Action and Contemplation
Albuquerque, New Mexico, USA

INTRODUCTION

Sometimes we just need to hear things from a different viewpoint, to see things from a different angle for an old message to strike us in a new way. That is especially true for the wisdom contained in the pages of the bible. Although it is increasingly the case that many in today's world haven't read those stories, there is nonetheless a perception that they are too well known to contain any surprises. For those who think they know these stories well and for those who have never read them this is the book for you.

Mark Townsend manages that difficult and challenging task of surprising us with what we think we already know because he himself has continually been surprised and opened up by both the harsh experiences of life and those friends and inspirers who have shed new light on his experiences by reading with him the timeless tales from the Christian scriptures. The process of being surprised, of opening up, is an indication that the God who was in Jesus continues to be in us, re-telling the tale that each matters, that no-one is beyond the reach of God, that nothing can impede the breaking-in of the non-accusatory forgiving presence of Jesus-Crucified-and-Risen and amongst us still to this day.

During Mark's decade-long ministry as an Anglican priest his sensitivity to and awareness of the mysterious and awesome nature of human experience gradually increased as he journeyed with his parishioners and himself through all the traumas and failings that are simply part and parcel of the human condition. He reveals an open transparency in which we can see and feel the wounds life has left behind, the scars that indicate where once he was hurt and where now grace has worked its magic. Forgiveness and acceptance bring peace and consolation and yet the memory is there of mistakes made and damage done to self and more distressingly at times, to others.

The gospels do not age and have the power to go on amazing us with their wisdom. They contain encounters that are extraordinary and also ordinary, a woman caught having illicit sex, an old man passing through the Temple, a soldier just doing his duty and a man walking away from his shattered dreams, a visitor from a distant land who has a once in a lifetime heart-stopping moment when he is held by the gaze of a new-born child, and a guest at a wedding reception dying for a drink! Mark brings these events to life and invests them with insights that come straight from his own experience. He shares with his readers what he once shared with his parishioners; a unique stance from where he understands anew both the gospel story and the human predicament. The effect is strangely beautiful in that it is at the same time both disturbing and encouraging, both unsettling and upbuilding.

Today Mark is concentrating on an aspect of his life that has always fascinated friends and enemies alike, his immense skill in connecting people with their unused and often undiscovered capacity for awe and wonder in the unexplained and the mysterious. He creates spaces in which his audience find themselves being transported to a place that entrances and engages and always leaves them begging for more. It is such a wonderful place to be, somewhere inside us that some hadn't visited before and others never knew existed, a place of astonishment and amazement in which something new happens, some new joy enters in and a smile begins its journey from deep inside to explode in radiant beams lighting up and transforming the face of each participant.

It is a magician's gift to engage with the spiritual and unexplained and Mark is one of the most gifted. As a magician Mark is well used to connecting people with their spiritual self and in this latest book he works his magic again. He introduces us into the company of some of the characters from the gospels and in so doing we are introduced to a part of ourselves, to a part of our story and are offered the chance to think afresh, to get a new perspective, to see another way through the events and experiences of our unique life.

If you enjoy this book you might want to find out more about Mark Townsend. You should visit his website at www.magicofsoul.com

and read his best-selling book *The Gospel of Falling Down: the beauty of failure in an age of success.* In his first work he maps out for the reader the simple truth that there is One who is waiting to catch us no matter how hard we fall, that our disasters and mistakes do not have the final word or the power that we endow them with. A new moment awaits, a new opportunity for growth and healing beckons. Mark knows because Mark has been there. These books come straight from the heart of one who despite everything that has happened to him is still alive to tell his tale!

Fr Gerry Proctor
Liverpool Hope University
Research Student.

The Magi's Tale

3 Gifts

Three wise men came from afar
or maybe much nearer.
Gifts were wrapped in gossamer words.

One knelt before me with gold in hand,
deep golden, like a hidden spring,
touched by the fingers of God.

The second gave me a shawl
to wrap round my shoulders.

The third held a sparkling wand
or was it a chiming chord
or yet a silver note or magic pen.
I cannot hold it still;
it changes like a chameleon.
It changes base metal into a fathomless seam of silver.

They lie before me, one, two, three gifts,
love given,
love received,
and longing transformed;
gold, embrace and transformation.

By Judy Dinnen (a poem that 'appeared' after reading The Gospel
of Falling Down)

He was a remarkable man, priest and politician, magician and
magistrate. Honored by our nation he became the most respected
of the 'King-Makers'. Truly great, he manifested pure inspiration
in human form. He was the personification of wisdom. Of course,
while still living, he would never have allowed me to speak of
him that way, but now welcomed into the next realm I can shout
it from the temple tops. At last I can tell his story, his tale of spellbinding enchantment.

We are The Magi. We are the keepers of secrets, the inter-
preters of dreams, the readers of stars. We are also the leaders of
the people. Centuries ago our role was purely spiritual, attached
to the Courts as magical advisers but, over time, our civic position
evolved.

Ever since the days of the great Jewish magician Daniel, we

Persians have been closely intertwined with the Jewish nation. Both suffered greatly under the Seleucids and both regained independence, the Persians as the major power within the Parthian Empire. This was the period when we Magi took on a priestly and governmental office. We had the privilege of choosing and electing our kings.

I myself am a novice. I have much to learn before I can officially call myself a Magi. I am a man with many more lessons to gain and examinations to pass, yet I've had such a great advantage for the last of the Great Ones was my teacher and Mentor. He was a wizard, a high priest and also a father. He was my father! I was not born from his seed but I became his spiritual son, though he chose to call me his 'little brother' for he was too humble to think of me his child.

My Mentor's greatest story was of the days before Rome had totally ransacked Judea. The armies were there as an occupying force, but the Jews were allowed to practice their religion without too much difficulty.

Back here in Persia my Mentor had been receiving 'messages' within dreams, haunting visions filled with both pain and beauty, fear and hope, hate and love. At the same time other wise Magi were buried deep in their own astrological investigations and were becoming more and more excited by the appearance of a new star. After many months of discussion, further exploration and the detailed interpretation of dreams, everything pointed to something truly wonderful - the birth of a new King, only this would not be a Persian king but a great Emperor of Universal significance. Can you imagine the excitement?

My Mentor and his brothers (now known as the Great Ones) set out in search of the king. Together with their entourage of soldiers and servants they traveled in the direction of Judea. The astrological maps pointed them in the direction of the great city of Jerusalem. He told me how, though the journey was long and slow, he was comforted by the accompanying star. It seemed to be guiding them as a comforting sacred presence.

They finally arrived at Jerusalem and, after having gained an uncomfortable audience with the Ruler, set off once more to find a small town called Bethlehem where the ancient Jewish prophets had foretold of a great king's birth. They journeyed on, grateful for the new information but troubled by the response of the Jewish King. There was a look of menace within him.

I will never forget my Mentor's facial expression when he described what he beheld in that little town on the outskirts of the great city. Though I know I have not the writer's skill I'll try to do him justice. He spoke many times of this encounter but it was the very first time that stays with me the most, the time he gave me *the Gift*.

We'd been discussing the nature of good and evil and I'd found myself confessing to him the many doubts I carried around with me. I also risked telling him that I often felt far from the ways of the Magi and that I feared a lack of what it would take to join their ranks. I told him how I often saw demons of darkness within my own heart and soul which would surely pollute the great Order of the Magi if I they were not purged out of me.

As I spoke he listened attentively, nodding occasionally and smiling gently. He created an atmosphere that allowed my words to flow out unstinted by any inhibitions.

Finally he looked into my eyes, 'My young friend,' he said, 'I want you to have a gift, a gift I was given many years ago.'

He put his hand on my forearm and squeezed it gently. I held out my hand to receive the gift but he simply smiled saying, 'I'll give you something tangible to hold in a moment. First let me pass on to you a gift that can be transferred directly to your heart.'

As he said those words I remember a shiver of excitement pass throughout my entire body. *What could he mean?*

'My dear apprentice,' he said, 'many years ago my brothers and I set out on a dangerous journey, a journey to find a king.'

He told of how the star, the visions and the scriptures had

eventually led them to the very house were he found the new king.

'What did you feel?' I asked.

'I felt as though I was about to enter a heavenly palace. I still feel the magic in my soul when I remember being welcomed through the door and seeing him for the first time.'

'Tell me, tell me what he was like.'

The old man closed his eyes and was silent for a while. I watched as his memories flooded back into his mind and transformed his complexion. He suddenly looked thirty years younger and the smile on his mouth was the look of paradise.

Then, eyes still closed, he said, 'My brothers and I entered the little room. It was the child's father who opened the door to us. He seemed to be expecting us. His face displayed no alarm at opening the door to a group of strange Pagan Priests. The second person I noticed was the mother. She sat in a chair holding a sleeping baby, face buried into her bosom. She looked so young, yet had a remarkable ageless wisdom in her eyes.'

'But what was *he* like?'

My Mentor opened his eyes and looked into mine as he said, 'He was like no child I'd ever seen before. The mother woke him for us. He was no more than a year old. We stepped forward and held out the gifts we'd taken for him. He smiled and, like his father and mother, also seemed quite un-phased. It was as if he was used to greeting strange people bearing gifts. I wondered whether we were just the latest in a long line of many.'

'Did he look at *you*?'

'Oh, how he looked at me. Yes, his mother placed him on the floor of the room. I knelt down and he crawled across the floor to me. This little king leaped into my arms and there I knelt for some time, cuddling the little bundle of royalty. He was more than a king though. We all knew that.'

'What do you mean?' I asked.

'I'm not sure but I know this, when I looked into his little eyes they held memories far older than their age. He was an ordinary little boy but there was something extraordinary about him too. Holding him was like holding onto something priceless and ancient. He came from above, of that I'm certain. Meeting him was the greatest gift I could have ever been given.'

My Mentor then stopped talking for a moment, raised his hand and, with one finger stretched out, pointed at me. His eyes widened as he said, 'This child holds a key to your own happiness my dear apprentice.'

My eyes now mirrored his, 'Go on, please, tell me what you mean.'

'You say you have been struggling with feelings of unworthiness, as if you don't have what it takes to be a good Magi. You fear you'll bring impurity to our Order. Well, my little brother, I felt exactly the same as you do before I met that little king.'

I was surprised, 'What happened to change you?' I asked.

'I don't know. I honestly don't know but it was as if this little one in my arms somehow oozed goodness, goodness that was unlike any other kind of goodness I'd experienced before.'

'Explain.'

'Often we meet *good* people don't we? We meet those who do everything right and who never seem to make mistakes. You must have others in your novice group who sometimes come across as totally perfect?'

'Yes. Yes I do, of course I do. They scare me. They're part of the reason why I feel so dark inside.'

'Exactly,' said my Mentor, 'Those outwardly good people make you feel like you'll never reach their level of purity. They bring all your feelings of darkness and evil to the foreground. Well, this little one was the purest goodness in human form, and his parents had a similar quality about them, yet none of them made me feel lower or different in any way. In fact they brought the good in me to the forefront. They enabled me to feel beautiful, special, like I'd never felt before, like I was a glittering diamond.

The goodness of this child was infectious, touching and changing all around him.'

'What happened to that child and his parents?' I asked.

'Oh you'll soon know his whole story and it will heal you like it healed me. You see many years later I encountered him again, through his story. He was not always able to share his goodness with others the way I saw him do. Those who were open to him were often the ones like you and I, men and women plagued by feelings of badness and corruption, but those who were the religious rule makers and law keepers feared him. They couldn't bare the thought that the unworthy were being set free without their own hand being involved. At first they just resisted him but finally they destroyed him. His gift was too great a challenge for them. My dear apprentice many of our fellow Magi have also resisted him for the same reasons.'

'Please, keep talking; tell me more of his story.' I felt a warm glow in the pit of my stomach, a warm glow of excitement.

My Mentor turned round and took hold of a small item wrapped in a gold and purple fabric. He handed it to me and said, 'There! Unwrap it. It's yours now.'

I can't describe the sense of wonder as I took it in my hands and started to remove the cloth cover.

'What is it?' I said, as I removed the scroll from its wrapping.

'This is the gift my dear one. It is His story, the royal child's story. It was written many years after he died. There were a few who attempted to record his tale. This is a copy of one of them. It is written in Greek, so you'll be able to understand it but you might need a little help in some parts. '

'But it's yours. Why are you giving it to me?'

'Because I'm old now. I don't have much time left. You need it more than me. You'll begin to understand things like never before once you read His story. He grew up and helped many people come to terms with who they are. He challenged those who thought they were good and embraced those who knew they were bad. He came with a message never heard before. He said 'love your enemies' and 'do good to those who hate you.' He encouraged folk to even love the enemies within themselves. You will, I promise, no longer be so full of self-doubt and unworthiness once you absorb his story.'

'Why haven't I heard of it before?' I asked.

'Because his story was feared and many men have tried to stamp it out of existence. He himself died a young man and though he had a handful of true followers they were not tolerated by the authorities. The only way folk could pass on his teaching was by illegal scrolls like this, and in secret meetings. I am convinced that one day His story will be known by the entire world.'

'Thank you.' I said, 'I will treasure this.'

I held the scroll to my heart.

'You will also learn to treasure yourself,' said my most wise of Mentors.

He died shortly after he gave me that scroll and every time I read from it it reminds me of him. And he was right; it contains the most remarkable words I've ever encountered. It holds more magic than the whole library of the Magi. It is spiritual dynamite and has brought me close to this child who was a king - this martyr who was a god. *He* has spoken through these words *to me* and has lifted me out of my own dark pit into his glorious world of light. *I am* a transformed man. I am a Magi but, more than that, I am a child of God.

All the Tales of this book are loosely based on certain passages, stories or parables from the New Testament section of the Holy Bible. The story of the Magi is found in Mathew's Gospel, chapter two.

The Tale of Old Mr. Righteous

Have you ever had an experience that leaves you dumbstruck with awe and wonder; a glimpse of heaven so profound that it becomes impossible to adequately describe? I had one not so long ago, but before I attempt to share it let me say something about myself. It'll help you to understand.

Ever since I was a young boy I've put all my will into living by the laws of Yahweh, following the commandments to the letter. Though it's so long ago I can still remember how, when the other boys would be off playing games on the dusty streets of Jerusalem, there I'd be with my head stuck in a scroll, sitting against a dirty wall, lapping up all those wonderful stories about my ancestors. I never found it a bore like the rest of them. I loved it, even the difficult bits. I don't know why, I just did.

This love for the traditions has never left me. I guess that's why all the people round here call me 'Old Mr Righteous'. They think I'm *so* devout, but they don't know what goes on in my head.

To be quite frank I never have found the laws to be too demanding. It's as if they come naturally. However, what I have found excruciatingly difficult is tolerating all those who do find religion a drag, a bore, irrelevant. I'm better at it now but as a younger man I had no sympathy for those who tried to follow the traditions but kept making mistakes, forgetting about the Sabbath laws and so on.

It sounds crazy but at times I felt so angry I could have stoned them. I saw them as so pathetic, weak and useless. I found it unimaginable that my beautiful traditions were not respected and loved *and obeyed* by all.

Oh, I've lost track of the arguments I've had, of the harsh and cruel things I've said to those who didn't agree with me. Dear oh dear, I've been so punishing. But we all go through periods where we get things wrong don't we! Don't we?

As I grew older this tendency to be rather punishing was tempered and I gradually became more tolerant of those who are different, though I've always believed that the scriptures and the traditions are the most important thing a man like me has to hold on to, and I still hold on to that *even after my experience.*

It was early last week and I was walking home. I'd been absorbed for the previous few days in the Holy Books and had read again about the Messiah. Oh how those words sent tingling sensations down my spine.

I was on my way home after visiting one of my brothers from across town, but something prompted me to take a detour past the Temple grounds. I don't know why but I knew I should follow the instinct. As I was walking I distinctly heard a voice; not anything audible but it was so strong I can only use the language of hearing to describe it.

Please believe me, I'm not one of those tiring people who hear angels talk to them on a daily basis, but I did hear a voice. Not words though, it was more like a sudden awareness, an injection of knowledge that came into my mind not via the senses but somehow directly. From that point on I knew I that was about to witness something, or see something, or even meet someone, very, very, special.

So I walked on towards the Temple, which was still quite a distance, and as I continued all those wonderful passages that I'd been engrossed with started to dominate my excited mind. Then I was sure, sure that I was going to see something, or someone connected to the Messiah, or could it actually be the Messiah himself?

I finally reached the temple Courts. It had taken quite a while to get there. I don't get around as easily as I used to you know. I was tired and I needed to rest for a moment so I found a quiet spot and sat down, still certain that something was about to happen but not sure what.

I remember how quiet the grounds were that day. The heat burned down and turned the sandy floor hot like a baker's oven and, being the temple grounds, the flies were dashing about frantically in swarms.

I waited and watched and waited.

Then I saw them, a simple couple with a young child in their arms. They were pacing slowly into the courtyard and making their way to the Temple steps. I knew they'd come for the ceremony of purification for they had with them a pair of doves. But why was I so interested in them? Certainly not because of their appearance or because they were in any way unusual, yet again that burning feeling told me it was them I had been led to meet. I got up and slowly made my way across the courtyard to make contact.

I'm going to struggle now because my feeble words are so incapable of describing what happened to me. All I can say is that for some unfathomable reason I knew it was not the parents but the infant they were carrying that was the one. Yes the one, the one indeed. This infant, this tiny, fragile being was the one I had been reading about all my life. This child, he was, he *is* the one who has been longed for by our people for centuries. I knew it. I was so certain. Don't ask me to explain why but believe me, trust me that I'm telling the truth.

So I greeted the little family and asked to be allowed to hold the child. For some reason they didn't object. It was as if they were used to people showing interest in their little boy.

I held him. I held him, this little bundle of prophecy. This was the one who we call Messiah. I, Simeon, Old Mr. righteous, held the Messiah in my arms.

I just held him, for ages it seems. The little chap was sleeping. He seemed so small, so dependent and so beautiful.

Then a wonderful thing happened. The little one opened his eyes and looked into mine. I was gazing into the eyes of my own salvation. But I saw something else in this little one's eyes. I saw not only my own salvation or the salvation of the righteous like me but the salvation of all those I'd been so punishing to over the years, all those who failed and had fallen and found belief so hard.

It didn't stop there! My eyes looked even deeper into his and I saw, for the first time in my entire life, that this salvation, this holy one who we've prayed for to come and deliver us from our enemies, is not just a gift to us but is also a gift to our enemies. This one, this holy infant, will be a light to reveal God's loving kindness to the entire human world.

I still can't believe I was holding this beautiful gift to us all.

When I eventually gave him back to his mother and blessed the three of them I was in tears; tears of awe and wonder, tears of pure joy, yet tears also of sadness. I don't know why but I felt this little one and his parents are going to face enormous pain in the years to come. Perhaps it was that strange and eerie shadow that I saw on the dusty ground as the child was passed to me to hold. It reminded me of a tree, a tree that is used for cruel and callous purposes.

But now I am a changed man. I haven't got long left in the

world, but however long it is I know I will be different from now on. Though I will continue to follow the ways I've followed for my whole life, I somehow now see them as really rather insignificant.

Do you understand? I've looked into the eyes of The One. I have seen my own salvation and I've discovered that it's nothing to do with what I can achieve, it's about surrendering myself to this God who (by some profound miracle) has paid us a personal visit.

Did I just say that? I could be stoned for less, yet it is the truth. Oh yes it is the truth.

The story of Simeon is found in Luke's Gospel, chapter two.

The Rabbi of Cana's Tale

It was a few years ago now, my glimpse into glory, and I happened to be conducting a wedding ceremony for a local couple. They were a beautiful couple and looked like a prince and princess.

As the Officiating Minister I was kindly invited to the reception. The bride was from a wealthy Merchant family so it was an extravagant affair. There were two great tents filled with tables of exquisite food and even a huge play area for children. There was exotic traditional entertainment in the form of dancers and musicians. There even a Fakir, a strolling magician with a snake basket and a magic flute. He seemed to be able to work real magic, with all his flashes of light and coloured smoke. It was amazing!

And then there were the guests: I tell you I've never seen so many people at a wedding reception, and from every place on earth it seemed.

There was no hiding the fact of the two families' importance. You could tell that by the sheer scale of the reception; the food, the wine, the guests, the setting.

I remember being introduced to both sets of parents. They were so kind about the wedding ceremony that I performed, and they showed me genuinely warm hospitality. But it was the bride's father who stood out. My God, what an impressive guy! There was something about him. I don't know what it was. All I can say is that he looked like a King.

Anyway time went on, and more guests arrived, and then something odd happened. For a moment it all went quiet. It was as if time had momentarily stopped. People stood almost frozen, facing towards one of the marquee entrances. I couldn't make out what (or who) it was they were gazing at.

Then, just as suddenly, the spell was broken and everything was back to normal again; the chatter, the laughter, the celebration, the dancing.

It was one of those occasions when time seemed to momentarily stand still. Has that ever happened to you?

A few more hours passed, the temperature was rising, a couple of guests were getting a little drunk, and the music and dancers were still working their visual and audible magic.

And then I saw his face, the bride's father. For a man like him to be looking like that something must have been wrong. He looked, how can I put it, as if the weight of the world had fallen upon his shoulders. As the Rabbi I thought I'd better go over and see what the problem was but I was more than a little nervous. He wouldn't talk.

I learned later that he couldn't face me out of embarrassment. Embarrassment! What had happened to make him so embarrassed? I'll tell you what had happened. I managed to pick up from one of the waiters that, a couple of hours before, a new guest had arrived with his mother, but he'd also brought a whole group of friends with him uninvited. Now, this in itself was no problem at all. The bride's father would have normally been delighted to welcome a hundred more unannounced guests. However, today was different. There'd been a miscalculation on the part of the wedding co-ordinator. He'd accidentally not ordered enough wine. They were approximately twenty gallons short.

Without the extra guests, the wine could have lasted a couple more hours (enough time for someone to go and collect the extra) but now there were about forty or fifty more thirsts to quench. They'd be lucky to last fifteen minutes.

The bride's father looked sick with worry. There was only one person tenser in the whole place, and that was the poor co-ordinator. Thankfully the bride and groom, and most of the other close family members, had not yet learned of the bad news so they remained in blissful ignorance, but how much longer before their day would also be ruined?

Can you remember I mentioned the feeling of time standing still? Well it was about now that another such experience happened. It was similar, yet different. I noticed some movement over near the water fountains. The co-ordinator had managed to rig up a very elegant looking fountain for hand washing with six shoots of water. It was spellbinding.

So there was this movement going on over near the fountain, and that's when the second strange experience occurred. This time it was not like a great pause in time, but a kind of tremor, a non-physical rush that seemed to bounce out from the fountain point like ripples in a pond. It only lasted a few moments, but I could feel a sensation running through me; a pulse, a heartbeat, a wave of energy, that's all I can describe. Strange isn't it. I don't know what it was but something had happened.

I'm coming to the end of this little story, and I've described two of the things that happened that day, each of which were kind of unsettling to say the least, but the third experience was to have an impact like nothing else I can remember.

You see, an hour or so after the feeling of those waves of

energy hitting me, I suddenly realized that it was now way past the fifteen minutes that I'd been told the wine would last for. I suddenly grew a little inquisitive and went to find the bride's father again. There he was beaming, holding a full glass in his hand. All those cares and worries were now completely removed from his complexion. He looked better than he had all day.

I saw the co-ordinator too, and likewise he looked relaxed and happy. What on earth had happened? Well, I can't answer that. I guess somehow they managed to get a super quick delivery, or even rustled up something from the exclusive manor house wine cellar. Thinking about it, it must have been the latter because everyone was saying how the wine had actually got better in quality as the night went on, and it was pretty good to start with.

I turned round, happy and relieved that the party was not going to end in anyone's embarrassment or shame, and found myself looking into what can only be described as the most remarkable, enchanting, love-filled, and all together gracious face I've ever seen in my life. I don't know who he was, or were he was from, or even why he was there. After all, he didn't seem to be elegantly dressed like the rest of the guests. But he stopped me in my tracks, and without even saying a word to him or hearing any words from him, I knew, I just knew that he was the reason why it had all worked out as it did.   For a moment I stood in silence and wide-eyed wonder. He was so human, yet he wasn't. He was strangely authoritative, yet there was no sense of judgement or threat in his eyes. He was special, yet he *made me* feel special.

I can't remember anything much after that. All I know is that I went home a changed man.

The story of the Miracle at Cana is found in John's Gospel, chapter two.

The Mother's Tale

This is a confession. My son came home last week and told me a story I did not believe. At first I laughed inwardly but, after he insisted he was telling the truth, I scolded him for his lies. I should have known better. I should have trusted my son. I should have also believed that God could and would use him like that. I hope, my God I so hope, he is able to forgive me.

It was late afternoon and hours had passed since I'd sent him out to fetch the provisions. I stood outside the front door watching for him. He'd never taken so long to fetch bread before. I was worried for his safety.

Then I saw him. He seemed to be walking as if in a dream. He was also carrying something; a basket. He'd only been for a few small loaves and a couple of fish. What was he doing with a huge basket? I stormed over demanding an explanation.

'Where have you been? And what's this basket?' I snarled.

Then I saw inside the basket.

'What on earth? Where did you get all that food from?' I cried.

The basket was crammed full of bread. I dragged him into the house and sat him down. The odd thing is he didn't look at all concerned. He was only twelve years old but was acting like he'd been drinking.

'What's wrong with you, boy?' I demanded, 'Come on I need to know, what's been going on?'

He was sat against the wall. I stood!

Looking up at me he spoke. 'Mother,' he smiled, 'I've just met the most amazing man.'

'What man?' I shouted, 'I sent you for bread and fish. Who are you talking about?'

'I don't know his name. I've never seen him before. Mother, please sit down and I'll tell you everything that happened.'

His sense of peace calmed me a little and I sat.

'I'd bought the food mother,' he said, 'and was on my way back home. I'd got as far as the corner near the old synagogue when I saw something in the distance.'

'What did you see?'

'I saw a huge crowd of people. They were far away and were walking up the hill. You know the one Mother, the hill where father used to take me with the sling shot.'

'What did you do, son?'

'I stopped and looked for a while but then a group of people came by and started walking in the direction of the crowd. I called out to them and asked what was happening and they told me they were going to listen to the Teacher.'

'You didn't go did you son. Tell me you didn't.'

'Mother I'm sorry but I wanted to see what it was all about. Yes I followed them.'

'Child I've told you so many times. Why don't you listen to me? These days are not safe. Anything could have happened.'

'I know. I'm sorry.' He said.

My son then went on to tell me how he'd arrived at the top of the hill and sat down with a group made up of thousands of people. They sat and listened to this man for hours. He told me how, even as a twelve year old boy, this teacher had said things that made him tingle inside. He told me that the teacher had made him feel special. He told me how this teacher seemed special himself, even sacred.

'Then what happened?' I asked.

'Well, we'd been there for ages and people were getting hungry. I had the bag of bread and fish but no one else seemed to have anything. Some folk started groaning and complaining. They started shouting at the Teacher, "Give us something to eat"'.

'Why son?' why did they think he could give them something?'

'I don't know. One minute they hung on every word of his, next minute they complained of hunger. It seemed like they thought he could make food by magic.'

'Don't be silly boy. So what happened next?'

'He raised his hands and asked everyone to be silent,' said my son, 'Then he looked round and asked everyone who had food to take it to him. No one seemed to have any because I was the only person who went forward. As I walked I looked round and I'm sure I could see some people hiding things. Then the Teacher caught my eye and he smiled.'

'Smiled? Ok, tell me what happened next.'

'One of his men looked at me and saw what I had in my hands.

He laughed and said "Teacher, this boy only has a few loaves. That's going to feed all these people is it? Huh!"'

'And what did he do'.

'Mother he thanked me and touched my head with his hand. Then he held out the food and said a blessing... '

'What then?'

'He gave the bag of food to his men and told them to feed the crowd.'

'What, five loaves and two fish?'

'Yes. He gave them the little bag and they took out the bread but it just kept on coming. I don't know how he did it but soon everyone was eating. Mother I can see you don't believe me but look, this basket was given to me afterwards as a thank you because I gave the bread and fish. Mother you know I didn't have enough money to buy this amount of bread.'

I exploded with anger, 'You disobedient and lying boy,' I shouted, 'how could you treat me like this? How could you lie like that and expect me to be fooled. You've stolen this bread and brought shame on us. Get away from me.'

My poor son looked at me through tears. I'd hurt my precious boy. I wish I'd have trusted him. I wish so much that I had. He got up and walked out of the house head hanging low.

I sat there for a moment considering how I might punish him but then I heard something outside. I went to the door and looked up the street. A group of people were walking towards me and they too were carrying a big basket, like the one my son had brought home. I dashed over and heard the news that excited my soul yet broke my heart.

My son! My poor son had been telling the truth. Not only that, these people told me what the Teacher had said after this great miracle feast. They told me how he'd stood with his hands on a small boy's shoulders and said, "Brothers and sisters, this has only been possible because of a boy. Learn from him. He gave me all he had. I could only do what I did because he first entrusted me with his gift. Know this: you all have gifts, some great and some small and they are all able to be used for miracles if you let me bless them.'

I eventually found my son and tried to explain. I hope he can forgive me. One thing is for certain though; I will never doubt him again.

We should always listen to our children, for our children are open to the wisdom of angels and the very voice of God.

The story of the feeding of the five thousand is found in all four Gospels, but the version with the boy is in John chapter six.

The Fisherman's Tale

People often say to me, 'Oh how I wish I'd seen what you saw'. Then they tell of personal tragedies or deep inner problems and claim they'd no longer have them if they were in my shoes. They seem to believe that those of us who were there when it all started have some sort of immunity to pain.

How wrong they are. I'm not free from trauma. I'm not free from fear, or doubt, or even depression. But what I do have is a memory that enables me to re-play certain things, *real things that have happened*, external occurrences that speak of internal truths. I replay them every once in a while and find it helps with my own suffering.

Let me tell you about one such event; one that continues to give me strength and hope. I'm certain it will do the same for you, if you allow it to become part of you.

It began a perfect day. Not a cloud in the sky. Waters of the great lake smooth like a satin sheet. The others and I were loading the boat for an afternoon's fishing. There's always so much to prepare, and we were so engrossed in our activity that we failed to notice him standing there. In our defence we weren't expecting to see him that day, but there he was, the teacher, stood on the deck beaming his infectious smile at us. He looked as radiant as the day and as calm as the waters.

What a contrast to the image of the same boat, the same men and the same lake some two hours later. It seemed to come from nowhere. We'd been fishing for a while when the teacher suggested we sail over to the other side, the far side, of the lake. Then he slept!

I guess the constant demands on his attention had worn him out. Poor thing! He couldn't get a moment's peace, but he was at peace in the boat. There he laid, eyes closed, breathing deeply, still wearing a gentle smile.

Crash! It came like the unexpected attack of a hostile force and hostile it was. I never believed weather could change so suddenly, but it did. The sky darkened as though some great gloomy canopy had been stretched out over it. The clouds looked down in a menacing way, twisting and contorting their grey black forms into angry eyes and furrowed brows. The winds were visible, like huge arms spiralling down from above, grabbing at the sea and throwing it at us.

For some reason Jehovah, it seemed, had shown up, and he was in a bad, bad mood. Meanwhile, the teacher just slept.

We were scared. I'll tell you, I thought we were going to drown. The battering from above was more than any of us had experienced before and then it got worse! A bolt of lightening struck the mast and it split in two, one half crashing down and piercing the far end of the boat. Now water rushed in. Why was he throwing fire at us? What had we done?

I leapt from my position grabbing at the remains of the sail, tearing off as much as I could. Then I dived towards the gaping hole with the intention of plugging it. Meanwhile two of the others frantically shook the teacher.

'Wake up! Wake Up,' they screamed, 'We're going to die. For

God's sake, wake up.'

I still can't believe what happened next. In fact it's only the scar on my chest, caused by the oar's blade, that keeps me from denigrating this story to that of a dream. He awoke! The teacher awoke from his slumber and for a moment looked at me. How on earth could a man, in such danger, surrounded by such terror, stand there with a face of calmness and peace. Hell, *he was still smiling*. Didn't he notice what was going on all around him? Didn't he notice we were about to drown?

Then he turned and looked out to the sea as if sizing up an enemy. He lifted his head to the heavens and, with a voice and words that still echo around inside my head, commanded the clouds, the winds and the lightening to stop. I too looked up, and I saw those faces, those angry snarling faces in the sky, begin to relax and fade until the grey blackness finally vanished. The great spiralling arms ceased grabbing and disappeared back up into the sky. And it was calm.

The boat was in tatters and the water seeped through the plugged up hole, but the danger was over.

He was incredible. He was a man like us, yet had power over the elements. He calmed the very rage of God. How, I'll never know. Why it happened I'll never know. But happen it did.

He spoke to us by simply asking a question; a question that also contained the answer, 'Where is your faith?'

Nothing else was said. Nothing needed saying.

Yes, people often say to me, 'Oh how I wish I'd seen what you saw', but they are wrong if they think it means I never suffer. No, I'll always be prone to trauma. I'm human after all. I'll certainly suffer loss again, and maybe a health problem, but I do now have that memory. I have a memory of an event that helps me to see that even though life is messy and storms will come and go, the teacher still sleeps inside all of us, and we have the ability to wake him up. He may not blow out all of the flames, or deaden all the pains but he will be there with us. Oh, be certain of that, he will be there.

The story of the storm on the lake is found in Mark's Gospel, the latter part of chapter four.

The Tale of Two Lost Sons

Son 1.

You know I wouldn't be here if it wasn't for Jesus. You see he invented me, me and my brother. He crafted a story, a parable about us. So in one sense I don't exist, yet in another sense I exist inside all people because the story Jesus told about me is a story about the little-me who lives inside all people. I think my brother would say the same.

Son 2.

Yes, I too was invented by Jesus and I too exist within all people.

In some people I am the dominant one, and in others it is my brother whose voice speaks loudest.

Son 1.
Our father has a voice too and his voice also lives within all people. His is the hardest voice to hear.

Son 2.
I am the little-me who gains attention by being so good and perfect that my father will love me truly. But I feel so insecure because of questions like, 'What if can't keep it up? What if I give way and allow my brother's reckless behaviour to dominate?'

Son 1.
And I am the little-me who sometimes walks away from my father's love because I think I can find a better experience *out there*. I'm going to tell you a story of when I did just that, when I went searching for treasure but found only pig food. Yet the search in itself brought me the greatest treasure I could ever have found. It's the story Jesus himself told about me.

Son 2.
It was a story about the *two of us*.

Son 1.
You're right. You can chip in too brother.

Son 2.
I will.

Son 1.
I never really *knew* my father. Well, on one level I did, after all I'd grown up in his home, but I never *really knew* him until I decided to leave him. It was a strange thing to do, impulsive! I remember

feeling there must be more to life, more to experience, more to taste, more to discover. So I decided to ask my father for all that would one day be mine, and to my amazement he agreed.

Son 2.
It amazed me too.

Son 1.
So I packed my stuff and was gone.

Son 2.
Sure you did, but you didn't have to live with *him* standing in that doorway looking out to the distance. Day after day he'd be there, hoping, longing dreaming that you come back. It was so painful to watch.

Son 1.
I know brother, and he knows how sorry I am for the pain I caused him, but I needed to do it.

Son 2.
Selfish is what you are.

Son 1.
Right again, but true to myself too. You, brother, are just resentful because you never had the guts to rebel.

Son 2.
You are wrong. It's just that loyalty to my father came first. It's not about guts. It's about what is right. Now get on with your story.

Son 1.
At first things were wonderful. I had enough money not only to

stay in some pretty cool places but also make some pretty cool friends. The trouble was I'd never been away from home on this scale before and I was naïve. I didn't see that some of them were taking advantage of me.

Son 2.
You fool. What did you expect?

Son 1.
To be honest I don't know what I expected. I just knew I had to do it. But then the rot set in. Not only was I beginning to feel ill from the poison I'd drunk it wasn't long before the cash dried up and the mates all disappeared. I was suddenly alone and I'm not exaggerating when I say I wanted to die.

Son 2.
You only had yourself to blame.

Son 1.
You're right again brother and I take full responsibility for that. I was an idiot, but who knows why we do these things?

So there I was, now homeless and hungry, and really quite ill. I had nowhere to go and no one to turn to. The very last thought on my mind was my father. As I said, I didn't know him. I thought I did, and I thought he'd be like any other father I knew *and disown me.* What I'd asked of him was the greatest offence. Betrayal is what it was. It was like me saying, 'father you are dead.'

So I looked around for a job and ended up working for a Gentile family on a pig farm. Hell I had to *live* with the foul snorting creatures.

Son 2.
You only got what you deserved.

Son 1.
Brother I'm not going to argue with you. Everything you say is right. You are totally justified in what your option is of me but we both know that our father thinks differently. Neither of us knew him, did we? Father is not a judge who deals out rewards and punishments but a forgiving parent who deals out mercy.

Son 2.
(Silence)

Son 1.
Time went by and I was ready to give up. I developed large sores on my body and was convinced those dirty pigs had infected me with something ghastly.

Then, one morning, I woke up after a vivid dream. It was an unusually peaceful night and the dream was of my father and his slaves. I suddenly remembered that he treated his slaves better than I was being treated on this pig farm. So I decided to escape and make my way back home. My plan was to beg him to allow me to become his slave. I even contemplated not letting him know my identity for I thought I'd stand a better chance if I somehow disguised myself. I was thin as a stick and had a much longer beard. It wouldn't have taken a lot to pretend to be someone else. I honestly thought my father would disown me.

Son 2.
I'll never understand why he didn't.

Son 1.
Dear brother we'd both got him wrong. I wish you could see that too. I began my journey, and all the way rehearsed my words. Even then I was planning my act. I gave up the idea of a false identity and settled for a full blown 'have mercy on me' show. It would have been an act, a sham. I had no real sense of repentance

or sorrow. I was sorry for myself but still looked out for 'number one'.

The journey home was long and hard, made worse by my weak and ill state. However, after a few days I could see my family home in the distance. My empty stomach began to twist and turn with worry and fear. Was I going to be right? Was my father going to see me as a traitor and cast me back out into the certain death of the wilderness, or was he going to see me as a potential slave? One thing I knew was that he'd forever see me as a dirty rat.

My home got closer and then I saw a figure.

Son 2.
Yes a figure indeed; our father still looking out of that door way for *you!*

Son 1.
It was. It was my poor father.

Nothing could have prepared me for what met me that day as I tumbled down the path and fell near the gateway in a hopeless heap of rags.

He ran out to greet me, arms stretched out in front of him. And when he reached me he helped me up. He hugged me and held me and peered into my dirty black eyes, and I tell you I have never seen such love.

I did not know my own father. I'd got him wrong. But when I saw him, and when he embraced me and kissed me, I melted in his arms.

That's when I can truly say my heart broke. That's when I can truly say repentance took place, after this unwarranted and unbelievable display of fatherly love.

My mother had died many years before. It was as if she was there too. The intermingled motherly and fatherly love all tied up in one person. Something changed inside me that day. I saw my father through different eyes.

I am still capable of acting in a foolish and selfish way. Sometimes I need to in order to come back again to that profound and deep love of my father. My father's love was so great that he allowed me to leave him. He was willing to let go.

Son 2.

I am envious of you. You had more given to you that day than I've ever had.

Son 1.

My father loves my brother the same you know. My prayer for him is that one day he truly believes it.

Son 2.

Jesus invented me and my brother, so in one way we are not real. *Yet we are real.* Each person has a part of us inside, the perfectionist and the rebel, the Pharisee and the Tax Collector, the saint and the sinner. Neither can make God love them by their good deeds or hate them by their bad. Both are loved equally and perfectly.

Son 1.

So, Jesus gave my brother and I as a gift to the world, a gift that can be discovered in a book found in many homes, yet a gift that can also be refused or avoided.

I avoided a gift by running away and seeking pleasure elsewhere. It's fun for a while but it doesn't last.

Son 2.

And I avoided a gift by failing to see what was right under my feet, a priceless treasure. Because of my law abiding goodness, I also felt superior to my brother and I looked down my nose at him when he returned crawling on the floor.

Both sons together.

We say to all who read these words, 'Go find the book. Blow the dust from its cover and discover the gift for yourselves.'

The story of the Two Sons is found in Luke's Gospel, chapter fifteen.

The Fallen Woman's Tale

People have often wondered whether Jesus' words were a condition: "Go and sin no more!" But even I, the recipient, cannot answer that. All I can do is re-tell my story and let that be a pathway into the mystery of Grace.

*

The scorching sun bore down on my unveiled head, my dark hair absorbing the heat like a slate. I was trapped by a pack of wolves... hungry wolves dressed as men. Robes of respectable elders covered up fangs and claws that lay beneath. They snarled, growled and awaited the signal to pounce.

I was a fly caught in a web and a hundred deadly spiders were toying with their prey.

I prayed for the first rock to knock me into oblivion. If it didn't then the heat surely would. My trembling legs were gradually losing sensation. My bent knees were cut and sore. I cannot describe the visions of hell that stampeded through my mind. I knelt there waiting, crying, regretting and dying.

Their hatred and disgust! My head was bowed low but God I could feel it. I could taste the scorn. Their glares of righteousness peered down upon the poisonous snake squirming at their feet.

I was in the wrong. I knew that, and according to the law should have expected *this*. The penalty for my actions was death by stoning but why was I alone? *Where was he?*

I wished it would start. A short sharp shock and then silence! I wanted the turmoil to end. But it didn't. Why? For God's sake why couldn't they just get it over with?

Again, I thought, where was *he*? Where was the other party of this unholy relationship? Why was I alone being held responsible? Of course I didn't want him to be tortured like this but why was it me who had to take all the blame? Why didn't he have to struggle inside a spider's web?

I knew why of course. It was because of his gender. After all God blesses men doesn't he? Oh the privilege of being born a man. But more than that, he was a man of respect, a man held in high opinion. What would the community say were his identity to be made know public? And I was the cause of his sin. I was the evil serpent who tempted him and was now being named the scapegoat for us both. I was the sacrificial lamb who would heal and sooth the fuming crowd as they hurled their stones.

I dared look up. I raised my head an inch and strained to catch an unfocused glimpse through the matted hair in front of my eyes. Something was happening. A man in a dark robe was walking towards me. My heart pounded like I'd been running from an enemy so I dropped my eyes again.

Then I felt the shock of pain as a hand grabbed hold of my hair and yanked so hard that I heard the sound of ripping.

"Agggh".

My God it hurt. The hand grabbed again and I felt myself being dragged across the courtyard like garbage. I was dumped down in a heap on another patch of dusty ground. I opened my eyes a fraction and noticed some blood in the sand. It slowly seeped out of the wound where the hair was missing. Red blood. A vivid symbol of the curse, the curse of women. Blood so sinful! Blood so vile! Why was blood viewed like this?

"The life is in the blood," they say, for blood is also spilled and animals killed to bring life.

Blood! Why did feminine blood speak of ugliness and impurity? And why is the colour red so deeply associated with looseness and impurity?

I could sense the crowd swelling and through my tears could see more black robes. They encircled me. A mob of men holding missiles of judgement prepared to send me to hell.

Someone called out, a male voice, harsh and angry, like the sound of a sword being sharpened on stone. I was too dazed to make out the words but I instantly looked up and there I noticed an oddity. A figure stood out. I was not the only person kneeling in the sand. This figure was dressed differently too. He didn't wear the elegant black robes of the institution. There he knelt as if disinterested with what was going on. One of the men was talking to him but he seemed not to notice.

I could hear the sound of my own blood pumping around my body like a flowing river. Soon that river would be set free and so would my soul. I longed again for the swift kiss of death.

Then everything went quiet, as if the world has lost the capacity to create sound. I watched as the kneeling man reached out an arm and to write in the sand. He was too far away for me to see what he drew. The faint sound of pumping blood in my ears was all I could hear.

Suddenly the sound came back and I could hear shouting. The men who encircled the kneeling man were demanding something but he just ignored them and continued to play with the sand.

I thought I saw his lips move. He didn't look up or pay the men any attention, but I was certain he had spoken.

What happened next was unfathomable! I saw arms rise, arms

that carried weapons made of rock. I grabbed my head with both arms and pushed it down to my chest, trying to shelter it from attack. I waited, but nothing came.

Then it began; the stoning. Thud! It missed me. I squirmed and shook with fear. Thud! Another one missed. They sounded as though they'd missed by some distance. Thud! Was I dreaming? Was I being gradually pulverised while a trance saved me from the pain?

Thud! So many rocks were being thrown but none were hitting their target. Was it luck or just a cruel tormenting game?

There I knelt, listening to the stones and boulders being thrown until once more there was silence. No not silence, it was another sound, a different sound, like quiet fading footsteps. I don't know how long I remained in that state of confusion and disbelief, but what I do remember is the sound of one more set of footsteps, and they were clearly walking towards me. I opened my eyes. My head was still hung low but I saw a pair of dusty, sandaled feet inches from my knees.

What on earth was happening?

For hours I had not looked directly up but something in me knew, something in me trusted, something in me, I can't explain. I followed the path from his feet, up his legs and body, to his chest and neck and finally to his face. Oh that face!

No words of mine can adequately describe his eyes. All I can say is that I've never looked into such eyes before, and surly never will again. They were like oceans of love. They oozed authority yet also tenderness, humanity and grace. They were the first set of male eyes I'd seen for years that did not contain fear and hatred.

Then he spoke, 'Daughter, who condemns you?'

I was still half dazed but his question prompted me to look out across the courtyard. They'd gone. There was no one there, just a huge circle of rocks and stones.

I looked back into his eyes, 'No-one, sir', I said.

Then he smiled with a smile that reached out and touched my

own face. It was infectious. His smile was impossible to behold without it transforming my own complexion. He clasped hold of me and lifted me up onto my feet and, through those smiling lips which he pushed close to my ear, whispered, 'And neither do I, go now and sin no more'.

At first I was stunned. Then I just melted and fell into his arms sobbing great tears of relief as years of pent up self-hatred and emotion poured out from my eyes.

He held me you know. This man, who I'd never seen before and who could only be from God, hugged me tightly. I was a woman who men had decided was too unclean to even look upon let alone touch, yet this angel from heaven embraced me. For the first time in years I felt clean, washed, purified, forgiven.

*

So, "Go and sin no more!" Did I? Was it conditional? Or if I did fall again would he once more lift me back to my feet?

In truth I cannot answer that. All I can do is share my story.

The story of the woman caught in adultery is found in John's Gospel, chapter eight.

The Traitor's Tale

Two thousand years! That's how long I've been vilified by the church. Two thousand years. How many of you, when you hear my name, feel a slithering snake slide across your foot? How many of you can't even say my name without also muttering the word 'traitor'? And how many of you have used my name as a weapon to bring shame on those who've betrayed you? Can you imagine what it's like for me to be the owner of that name?

I loved him you know. I loved the Teacher. He drove me mad at times with his strange priorities but I adored him. For those three years he brought meaning to our lives. We were not an easy bunch to live with. Boy did we have our characters; Peter with his quick temper and tendency to act before thinking, Thomas with his analysing and sceptical mind, James and John with their arguments over which one's the greatest. Oh, He had a lot to cope with. But he loved us all, and we loved him.

Then things started to go wrong and I tell you I was so confused. It wasn't turning out like we'd expected. The people didn't seem to understand what the Teacher was trying to do and I had my doubts. Then fear crept in. I was terrified. He was walking into a snake pit of his own making and dragging us with him. God, someone had to do something, otherwise we would have *all* been nailed to a wooden cross.

So I, well you know the story don't you, but believe me I thought I had no option. It was like hell, yes inside my own head was the devil from hell and I had no power over him. Have you never heard voices in your mind? Have you never had doubts that lead to wrong actions? Have you never acted out of nothing more than pure self-preservation? If you have then you also know the crippling guilt that sticks to your soul like a thousand hungry leeches.

I saw the man I'd followed for three long years suffer like a dog, *because of a selfish mistake I made*. I saw him, I saw what they did to him. I wanted to scratch the lips off my face, those traitorous pieces of flesh that kissed him into oblivion. After that I did what anyone would do and for a moment the rope and branch relieved my mental turmoil, but only for a moment, for death is never the end of the story.

Since then many have assumed that I now live in the flames beneath the earth, a resurrection to eternal punishment for the sins committed against the Son of God. Sometimes I wish that were the case, for never a day passes without me looking at my reflection and wanting to spit. But that was not His choice for me and *this* is the real reason for these words.

I learned more about my Teacher in those moments following his betrayal than for the whole of the three years I lived in his presence. And I now want to share what I learned because I do not think I am alone. I may be the only man in history whose name has become synonymous with Traitor of the Son of God, but I am not the only man who has betrayed the Son of God. One reason why people hate me so much is that part of them hates also the unrecognised traitor within their own hearts, and it's much easier to have an external enemy than an internal one. I don't mind being their scapegoat. I see it as my vocation, but I also can be their Teacher.

I have something that may be of use. A lesson can be learned from my mistaken path.

Come with me, once more, to the upper room and sit down at that glorious Passover table, and watch. This was the night on which my name turned sour. I can remember it now. There we were sharing our final Passover meal together. Each one of us preoccupied by our own thoughts, wondering, contemplating what was going to happen?

Then the Teacher rose from the table, took off his cloak, and fetched a bowl of water which he placed on the floor in the bigger room. He called to us and made us stand around the bowl with our Teacher kneeling in front of it.

The first person forward was Peter, who looked in horror when he realised the Teacher was going to wash his feet. It was a typical Peter response, but he gave in and was washed by our Master. I stood there wondering and waiting and watching. I can't begin to describe the turmoil in my mind. This man was demonstrating more humility and love in those actions that I'd ever seen. We were his followers, his servants, yet he reversed roles and became, for a moment, our slave.

I stood hypnotised by the scene and terrified because my turn was coming. I knew he knew. I could see it. So will you believe me if I say that he washed my feet that night? He did. This broken messiah looked into the eyes of his own betrayer and washed his feet. Did you here me? Jesus washed Judas' feet. He cleansed the unclean one, he forgave me before I'd even done what I was about to do.

It has taken me the last two thousand years to realise the full significance of this. At first I created my own hell and condemned myself to exist in self-imposed judgement. But gradually, over time, after re-playing and re-living those events (in my mind) I have been able to accept His forgiveness.

Judas's story is scattered through the Gospels but the betrayal scene can be found in Luke's Gospel, chapter twenty two.

The Centurion's Tale

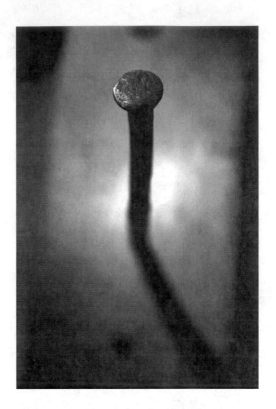

I will not blame you if you cannot make it to the end of these words. Certainly my story is one of the ugliest of all. Consider, for a moment, what would you imagine to be the foulest act a man could commit against his God? What crime would you label the most gruesome blasphemy? Whatever your imagination provides I'm sure that it cannot compare with my own great sin. I am the apostate of apostates... the sinner of sinners... the malefactor par excellence... *I am the murderer of the Son of God.*

We soldiers knew something was different about him. From the very moment he was brought to us and handed over by his own people we knew he was distinct. But we didn't know why.

Hell, if we did do you think we'd have done what we did to him? If we knew his true identity would we have pushed those bastard thorns into his head like that? Would we have scorned him, mocked him, flogged him until his shredded skin hung in ribbons? It was one of the darkest days I can remember. I can still see the fear written across the faces of my colleagues as the sun disappeared and the black blanket of death wrapped itself round us.

I was the one you know. I was the one who was given charge over his execution and, I have to admit, I made sure we did a good job. You have to understand this man meant nothing to me. He was just another troublesome Jew who should have known better than to stir things up. He was not of any importance. His crucifixion should have been of no consequence. God he was just some unheard of peasant from the Northern Territory. Why should I have cared a damn? Yet his memory has haunted me ever since.

That dreadful day was the first day I'd set eyes on him. I'd not even heard his name before, but the commotion he caused was like nothing we'd ever witnessed. From absolutely nowhere a storm kicked up among the Jews and before we knew it all Jerusalem was in a frenzy. The first image I had of the man was seeing him led out in front of the screaming crowds and presented by the Governor. He'd already been sent to his King, who clearly cared so much about his own that he simply rejected him and handed him back to the Governor.

Oh their hatred, their cries of damnation. What had he done to cause such offence? Whatever it was none of us understood, neither did we give a shit. He was 'just another bloody Jewish subversive' to us and I was, personally, more than happy when he was handed over to me and my own men for the 39 stripes. God we were brutal. When I think what we did, and what I now know about him. He was small and physically weak yet bore it like no man I'd ever seen. The lashes would have been enough but we didn't stop there. I have to confess I laughed when my men spat and pulled hair from his chin and beat him so hard that the leather sunk deep into his olive skin.

After that he was led back out to face the crowds. He was a piece of butchered meat. He was prey to a pack of wolves. He was a victim of the mob yet he said nothing to neither defend himself nor scorn those who abused him so. It was at this point that he started to unnerve me.

Once more The Governor presented him to the crowds and, to our shock, they still demanded his life. *Who is he?* The questions circled my mind like mosquitoes searching for somewhere to sting, but no answers came… just more questions.

The road to the hill top was long, made slower by all the strength that had been sucked from this rejected king. As he paced his way, each step looked like it was going to kill him, the huge weight of wood hanging over his shoulders like a shady symbol of death. My men still taunted him. They laughed, geared, whipped and spat and, as I watched, the more uncomfortable I became.

When we reached the top the man fell to the floor in what must have been a state of half relief yet half dread at what was to come. I ordered the soldiers to turn him over and begin the process. Hell this is hard. I can see him now. He was in such pain, yet still he said nothing to defend himself. He was remarkable. By this time I could barely watch as they stretched him out on that wooden rack and when the hammer was raised I winced and turned away. The dull thud was swiftly followed by a blood curdling scream. It was like a thousand blades running across slate at the same time. My men laughed as they drove in those torturous metal spikes. They laughed! The cross was then raised up and that poor man's pinned up body hung from the wrists. The body weight pulled downwards and the man yelped as the wounds tore a little more. I'd seen it all hundreds of times of course but somehow this was different, *he was different.*

Eventually the tree stood upright, between two others, each

one decorated by its own criminal. Criminals! Yes *they* were criminals but what about him? What had he done to deserve this?

One of them started shouting poisonous abuse at him but, incredibly, the other one reacted in his defence. I can remember it so clearly.

'Shut up! Stop saying that you bastard! You known that you and I deserve this shit but what has he done. Nothing. Look at him you foolish idiot, can't you see he's innocent?'

Then a remarkable thing happened, the criminal spoke to the man he had defended and whispered something I could hardly make out. It was something about paradise. I couldn't hear the reply either but something was said. However it's not the words that stick in my memory so much as the expression on the innocent man's face. Never in all my days have I seen anything like that. He gazed at the repentant criminal like, like a bloody mother gazes down into the eyes of the baby in her arms. His look was filled with compassion, protection and suffering love.

The peace didn't last long though for then the others started hurling abuse. Roman soldiers, Jewish bystanders, ever the High priest himself came up and spat at him. I did hear his words as the Priest turned and walked away; they were loud enough for all to hear; loud enough for the Priest to hear.

He stopped, eyes wide open as the suffering man said, 'Father forgive him, and forgive all of them for they don't know what they are doing?'

Again it was incredulous. He forgave the very people who put him on that monstrous cross. He forgave us all. He forgives Jerusalem and Rome, State and Religion, Temple and Palace. He forgave those who'd butchered him. He forgave me. That's when I knew we'd got it wrong.

He didn't last long after that. I think that act of forgiveness cost him the last few ounces of strength. He shouted out something I could not understand, bowed his head and that was it. At once the ground groaned and a clap of thunder cried out from the heavens above. The very earth we stood on was crying. The wind moaned like a thousand bereaved women.

'Surely this man was a son of the gods', I whispered into the wind. A Jew standing near heard me and nodded.

Since that day I've never slept without seeing that man's face. I'm not haunted by him so much as accompanied. I regret what we did to him. Oh yes. But I know that he forgave me. He forgave the foulest crime anyone could do to the God of the Universe. Did you hear me? He forgave the murderer of the human face of God.

My Centurion's story was based on a character found in Matthew's Gospel, chapter twenty seven.

The Tale of St. Thomas

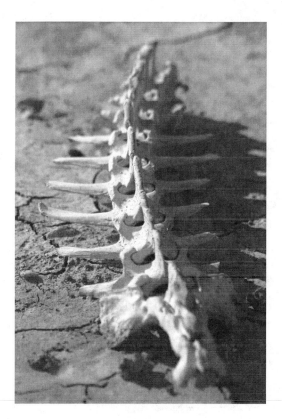

I once *saw* God himself. I saw him and I touched him. I looked into his eyes and gazed into his agelessness. This human face of God had the complexion of a young man yet wore a wisdom older than the universe. I'd seen him many times before of course, but not like this. He looked the same in every way yet he was different.

I am the one they called the doubter. I was born a sceptic and grew up with a mind that wanted answers; 'seeing is believing' was always my motto. But on that day my pessimism paved the way for the reception of a truly priceless gift; a gift that still feeds me with faith.

Up until then I'd been a troubled soul. We'd spent near on three years with the Teacher, yet I still found it difficult to accept that he was the One. The stories *he told* were powerful and moving, and had the ability to transform minds. But the stories that were told *about him* began to get exaggerated and stretched. I feared we were in danger of deluding ourselves into making him something he wasn't. So I became the rational voice of the group. I probably drove the others crazy with all my questioning and analysing but it's how I was made.

I *wanted* to believe like the others, truly I did. I wanted to have the faith to witness signs and wonders but it always turned out that I was at the wrong place at the wrong time. And even on those rare occasions when I was there I just didn't see it the way the others did. Cephas once claimed that he'd walked a few paces on the surface of the great lake but that's not how I remember it.

It's a damn curse you know, to have a mind like mine. It make's you the odd one out which is such a lonely place. And it can drive you mad, the incessant whirling of thoughts, the constant chattering of the inner debate.

Yet my mind can also be a blessing, as I found out so dramatically on that incredible day.

We were all together. It was a week since the others had claimed they'd seen him. I believed that *they* believed they'd seen him, but in my opinion it was self-delusion. You have to understand I'd seen his body after they'd brought it down from the cross. The man was dead. No one could have survived that ordeal. So when my brothers and sisters made these claims there was no way I was going to accept them. 'Seeing is believing,' I said to them, 'I will not believe, *I cannot believe*, until I see for myself.'

Well we were all together again. The doors and windows were locked because we were now targets of the authorities. It had been one of the hardest weeks of my life. Not only was I dealing with the huge sense of bereavement, and not only was it terrifying to be on the Temple guards' hit list, but now the closest people in my life had all lost their minds. I just wanted them to grow up, or shut up. I wished I could have shaken them out of their dreams... knocked some sense into them. I felt lonely and frightened. I didn't know these people anymore.

There we were... me and them... all together, yet so far apart.

'Thomas,' said the quiet whisper of a voice.

'Thomas,' I knew the voice but it couldn't have been.

'Thomas, peace be with you. Peace be with all of you.'

I could not believe my eyes and rubbed them hard but, on opening them, he was still there. He was standing there, my Teacher.

He walked over to me and held out his hands. I could see they were still wounded. Instinctively I reached out and touched. He didn't seem to mind. He always knew I needed proof. Then he took my trembling hand and placed in inside his robe and I could feel where the spear had been driven in. I withdrew my hand and held it in front of my eyes... blood. It was real. *He was there.*

At that point all I could do was drop to my knees and weep. I wept for many reasons: Guilt! I'd been part of his betrayal. I saw what they did but lifted no hand to help. Unworthiness! The others knew he was risen yet it took this to convince me. How could he love a man who lacked faith like this? Emotional pain! The pent up feeling of sheer loss now poured out as the rivers ran down my cheeks. But as I wept a cleansing seemed to take place and my tears gradually changed from self pity to joy. My eyes cleared and I looked up at him. There was no look of anger or punishment in his eyes, just compassion and love.

I knew then who it was I knelt before. For the first time in my life I knew.

'My Lord and my God,' I said, not knowing where the words had come from.

I was the first to know this fact, *that he was God*. I still find that an amazing thought, that it took an old sceptic like me to recognise the true nature of Jesus. The irony is that my doubt has now led to many others' re-awakened faith. My questioning mind has enabled dry bones of faith to live again. Over time, of course, I discovered that what I saw so brightly in Him is also in us - that we are all part of the Divine. The genius of the Teacher was that he somehow re-directed our gaze and pointed us back to ourselves. When we saw the God in him, he reflected the light, like a mirror. Then we were able to see the light, the light of God, in us.

Thomas's story is found in John's Gospel, chapters twenty and twenty one.

The Disillusioned Disciple's Tale

It's a glorious spring early evening. There's a gentle breeze and the descending sun creates the most beautiful patterns in the sky, but the beauty of the surrounding only makes the ugliness of the situation more difficult to bear.

You feel shocked, stunned and bitter and, as you and your companion slowly walk towards the setting sun, you try to make at least some sense out of the hell of what's happened. But you cannot – there's only darkness. You talk about how things were before the stranger from Nazareth came. You remember the utter hopelessness; the working of such long hours for money that was sucked up by the Romans as Tax; the fear of living in an occupied territory, a fear that has returned.

The fear itself reminds you of the temptation you always had to join the underground, but you'd always been put off by the countless tortured bodies that were hung up on crosses as a perverse deterrent for would-be subversives.

Your companion now speaks. He talks of how The One had

changed your lives. How He had given a brand new vision of what life could be like, and how He had bought you to a place where you were not only able to forgive your enemies, *but yourselves.*

For a while the memories lighten things but soon you both plunge back into the darkness as you cry out simultaneously, "Jesus, why did you get it so wrong. Why did you die?"

You plod on, heads hung low, in silence and gloom.

As you walk, your mind continues to play back the haunting memories of the callous events. You watch it all over again and again. How He never lifted a finger to protect himself. How He was beaten and sworn at and finally nailed to that disgusting tree. How He was taken down, bound and hidden away behind that colossal rock.

But that was three days ago. Now your thoughts move on to earlier on *this* day, when Mary and a friend had told you that pathetic story about Him being alive again. You 'tut' to yourself, and shake your head as if to shake off their superstitious and childish nonsense from your 'superior' mind.

Now you are about half way to your destination, but you realise someone else has joined your company. He is a stranger and he could have been with you for quite some time, so deep were you and your friend in your own thoughts.

After a while He speaks and asks what you have been talking about. At that you all stop and the two of you look at him, your faces betraying your inner agony and despair. "You look as though you've lost everything," He Says, "What has happened?"

Your companion speaks up: "Are you the only man coming from Jerusalem who does not know what's been happening?" And, due to the stranger's response, the whole story pours out like a river of tears from the eyes of a man who's just learned how to cry. You sob, the river flows, and the pain is slowly eased.

But then you reach the part in the story where the women claimed that Jesus was alive again, and your face now betrays another emotion, embarrassment.

And now the stranger talks. He talks about your beloved scriptures, and as he does so he expounds them and you feel your toes beginning to tingle and your heart beginning to warm. He talks on, and his words and ways seem familiar, yet you cannot put your finger on it.

Now your heart is burning.

The first half of the walk to Emmaus had seemed like a lifetime, yet now you have arrived at your destination and the time passed without you noticing.

You and your companion begin to turn off into a path leading to a little village Inn, but the stranger continues on his way. You call out to him "Sir, the day's almost over, please come and stay with us at this Inn". You are inwardly overjoyed to hear his response.

You are now at the table in the Inn. The stranger does something rather odd, He reaches over to take some bread. Part of your thinks this is wrong because guests never take bread first, but another part of you didn't think it was wrong at all, in fact it seemed prophetic.

Now He is holding the bread in both hands and he begins to say a blessing (a blessing that sounds familiar, but you can't put your finger on it). The bread now breaks and the stranger holds out a piece for you and a piece for your friend.

You reach out to take the bread and look down into his hands and what you see makes you shudder, the stranger's hands have wounds, nail marks. Trembling, you slowly let your eyes travel from his hands up to his arms, across his shoulder and to the face that you thought you'd never see again. The man is no longer a stranger.

You now sit half in shock and stare into the face of Jesus. He looks at you with an expression that is impossible to adequately describe, except to say it contained a mixture of love and power, compassion and friendship.

You reach out your own hands in amazement wonder and awe, and He vanishes from your sight, but the broken pieces of bread lay on the table as a testimony to the fact that it was not just a dream.

The joy starts running through you as though a great spiritual dam has burst and released a huge currant of pent up energy. You feel like you've been carried right into the very heart of God's love.

You don't feel sad that He has gone once more for the disappearance this time is not an end but a great new beginning. His disappearance is, to you, an essential part of the Gospel of Grace, for it means He is now always present. You know now that He *was* present all along the dark road to Emmaus, *even* before He actually walked beside you. And you know He will be with you for now and for ever and ever.

You look at your friend, Cleopas, and he looks back at you. No words are necessary. All you know is that you *do know* and every time you break bread again you will also *know*. Thanks be to God.

The story of the road to Emmaus is found in Luke's Gospel, chapter twenty four.

The Magician's Daughter's Tale

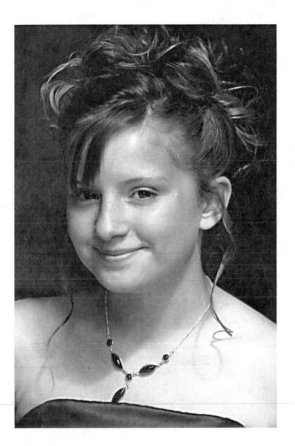

I began this book with a story about a real Magician, one of the Great Magi who held the Holy Child in his arms. So let me close where I began, back in that Bethlehem home.

A couple of decades ago I had the wonderful experience of visiting the Church of the Nativity in Bethlehem. It is a great basilica built on the traditional site of the Magi's visit to the infant Jesus. It was the 7th of December 1988, the run up to Christmas and, if one time of year has ever given me goose bumps of enchanted anticipation, Christmas is it. I guess it all fits in with my love of magic. Since early childhood I've experienced Christmas as thoroughly spellbinding time of year. The dark nights and colored lights, the brass bands and Carols playing in shops and arcades, the frosty weather and Santas on sleighs, I love it all. Each ingredient adds to the atmosphere of excitement and wonder. I believe we *need* a sense of wonder, mystery and enchantment in our often over-serious 'grown up' lives. We need to have the flickering flame of our long forgotten childlike imaginations re-kindled so we don't lose touch with our inner child. Of course this inner child is wonderfully far less immune to the contagion of Jesus than the rational adult of our normal personas. My experience that Christmas, as I sat in the belly of Bethlehem's great Temple to Jesus, was one such experience of divine contagion.

I had tried three times to get to Bethlehem. It was the anniversary of the intefada, so things were more than a little difficult, and my two previous attempts at catching a bus from Jerusalem to the 'little town' were obstructed by strikes. However, my third attempt was a success. The short journey took me past the little hamlet of Bethany and out into the Judean hills. As far as I recall the whole trip only took around half an hour - perhaps even less. I got off the bus and stepped into a market square. There were armed soldiers everywhere but the Church was right there. I entered the tiny little door in the front of the ancient building and passed through a huge basilica. After a little search I found another doorway and a passage with steps down to some sort of crypt. It was clearly the way to something special for there was a constant flow of people coming out from the passage.

I climbed down the stone staircase and found myself entering a magical world not unlike the Christmas Grotto set up in an old English mining cave that I visited with my wife and children last Christmas, though there was a tangible difference to *this* 'Christmas grotto'. Of course, it should not need saying that at the heart of the Christmas story is not a fantasy or a magical fable but a real story about a real human family who, like all of us, had to face real human concerns. It is a story of physical exhaustion, homelessness and human birth in the most unprepared and all-together unhygienic of labour wards.

But there I sat, on a ledge inside the holy cave, and watched as pilgrim after pilgrim brought their gifts to the symbolic place of Jesus' birth. Some brought candles, others brought coins, and still others lay on the floor and kissed the gold star marking out the divine birth place. It was like watching the Magi bringing their gifts. From every corner of God's green earth they came. It was pure enchantment. I remember thinking about the first Christmas and wondering what the actual Magi had been like. I also wondered about the parents of Jesus and then the infant himself. What an awesome image this is... this first picture of the saviour's birth. It is an image so powerful because it is about God plunging himself into our messy, confusing, painful and thoroughly human lives, our thoroughly imperfect human lives.

Try to imagine the scene: a baby born in rural isolation, far away from home, far away even from the Inns and hotels of Bethlehem... and not even given adequate shelter. A baby in a manger! Drop the sweet and sentimental Christmas card images for one minute. Let's remember what a manger is . . . *An animal food troth*, not a cozy hospital cot. Look again at the image. Where was the baby born? In a stable, probably a cave used for a stable on the outskirts of Bethlehem, and, apart from the parents, whose were the *first eyes* to see the baby? Not the angels, not the shepherds, not the wise men... no... the animals... what an amazing thought. The first eyes to set sight on the king of all creation (apart from Mary and Joseph) were the eyes of the ox and the ass, the donkey and (probably) a rat or two... THIS is a truly amazing act of God. He comes into the shit and squalor of our human and real and often messy lives and says 'You are so special that I chose to become one of you. This world and all it's people are so valuable that I will be born among you as one of you, and I will spend the next 33 years teaching you how special and loved you are to God. And even when some of you get frightened by my message and destroy me by nailing me to a tree, I will come back with the same message. . .

Christmas is about God reaching down into the hopelessness, the pain, and the dirt of the human situation, and becoming part of it. It is not about the birth of a new denomination or even religion. No! It's far bigger than that; it's about the bridging together of the whole human family and God. The message of Christmas (that rightly deserves all the extravagance of tinsel, turkey and trees) is the earth shattering and spine tingling good news that God is with us in person.

But, before I close with the final sentence of this collection of factual and fictional fables, let me introduce you to two more people – one real, one imaginary. My daughter, Aisha, is an amazingly inspired young girl of 14 years. In fact her creativity with words often makes me feel rather inept as a writer for her skills are already far superior to mine. She is also a free thinker. I have always encouraged that in both my children. Aisha considers herself to be of no "boxed" faith but loves the morals of Christianity, the wisdom of Buddhism and the connection with nature associated with Paganism.

I have invited her to quietly close this book in a way only she could, with her own unique brand of poetic wisdom. I asked her to conclude this Bethlehem story, which she agreed to as long as she could do it her own way. Well, of course I agreed, and so she came up with one more character for this book – the Shepherd Boy. This is *his* Tale through *Aisha's* imagination.

The humble, dusty town of Bethlehem lies nestled snugly between the softly sloping Judean hills. You walk slowly along the narrow labyrinth of unswept, sandy passageways and you come to a modest inn built of baked clay.

You can hear the soothing chirp of crickets, both close and

distant, filling the otherwise silent air, and you touch the oily wool of the lamb you have brought with you on your back, its cold head hanging limply over your shoulder. You choose the back passage as you notice the faint glow and flicker of a lamp coming from the room at the back kept for the animals.

But why is there a light in there for the animals? Animals don't get scared by the dark like humans; they have no need for light. You can feel the warmth escaping through the cracks in the door. You knock and a pleasant but drowsy voice comes from within. You enter cautiously with the feeling of complete enrapture. The door creaks slightly as you enter the room like in many houses but what you encounter is overwhelming. A woman with a weary but angelic face looks up at you with eyes that are the color of hazel nuts and are soft and dewy. Adhered in her arms sleeps a little baby, the color of olives, wrapped in an array of old sheets and blankets. He is just a typical infant but he has a sense of wonder about him that cannot be described.

You ask for the baby's name. The mother answers, 'Yeshu'. Her name is Miriam. She invites you to sit down but you stumble for you are still taken aback by the boy, Yeshu. The baby stirs a little from its slumber but settles gently back into the folded blue gown. You can smell the sweet breath of cattle and you can hear the mule's braying. And the sight of the baby is so holy that you feel you must offer something to the parents, suddenly you remember the lamb and swiftly you present it to Miriam. She smiles and thanks you and blesses you for she knows that your lambs are your livelihood and that such a present is a big sacrifice.

But you know that the child born on that night is something extraordinary and it would change your life and the lives of humankind forever and ever. Rejoice, Emmanuel is born, rejoice.

The story of the birth of Jesus is found in two Gospels, Matthew chapters one and two, and Luke chapter two. Matthew's contains the Magi, and Luke's the Shepherds.

EPILOGUE

So this little book has come to an end, but the tales, myths and legends of that remarkable first century radical continue. One of the wonderful things about the Bible is that it is a living, breathing, growing book. It expands as we read to take us deep into its stories, myths and treasures. When we choose to read it with openness and imagination it inspires, challenges and re-enchants us to life. However when we read it as the literal and authoritative 'rulebook' of Churchianty it reverts to being nothing more than just another Christian tool to segregate and make the so called 'true believers' feel superior. It's interesting that it is the 'superior' and 'religiously right' characters of New Testament are always the ones who receive the sharp edge of Jesus' tongue? It is the messy and muddled, the flawed and undervalued who get everything wrong who end up face to face with Grace.

The Bible works because it speaks directly into our situations and experiences. Tell me, who has never felt like one of the two lost sons or the woman surrounded by wolf-like-judges? Is there one person who has never doubted God or felt like a betrayer? What I have tried to do in this little book is demonstrate how we can read our modern day, and often messed up, lives into those ancient stories and by doing so gain new insights.

Sadly, at this very time of writing there seems to be a powerful conservative backlash in various parts of the Church as if the 'true way' is to revert to that old rule book mentality. I fear for its spirituality. The spirit is a flowing stream and requires freedom and openness within which to work. Yet when a river's pathway is blocked it will find other, more unconventional, ways to break free.

What you have just read is a revised version of the last of

three books I wrote as a full time priest of the Church. Each of those books marked a different stage in my journey as a stipendiary clergyperson. That particular journey is now over. I may come back to it some day, but if I do it will have to be me as I am, rather than me as the Church thinks I should be. I now stand, with excitement and fear, at the place on the river bank where the pent up water has escaped to form a new stream. I am preparing myself to dive in and see where it might lead. It is a mystical current that will carry me far away from the world of institutional religion but the one who's Tales we've just told is standing next to me and, I know, will be swimming with me. The Christ lives both inside and outside institutions, structures, temples and traditions and as I now journey on to places wonderful and weird, he comes with me.

I want to close now with some words from an email I send to my dear friend and spiritual sounding board, Rev. Caroline George:

'Life is still really tough Caroline. Every day flies by with so much to do and still hardly any cash coming in to pay the mortgage, rent and bills etc. But I'm free - OH GOD I'M FREE - freer than I've felt in thirty years. I can't express how frightening and at the same time how liberating all this feels.

Caroline, something's happening to me. It's as if I've entered a new stage in my magical journey, and it's rapidly moving me out of institutional / organized religion altogether and into something totally different... and yes Jesus is coming with me (because he's not the property of the Church).

I am feeling my dried up wells of the last few years of life within the dear old C of E (which I still love so much) beginning to be re-filled with living water, and it's tastes fresh and magical. I'm not sure where all this is leading but I know I need to let go and trust in the path – the Path of The Blue Raven*.'

Note: The Tale of where this river leads will be told in book number 4, The Path of The Blue Raven. The Raven is a powerful symbolic totem animal within many cultures and traditions. It marks new beginnings and inspires us to travel into the dark places of our own psyches to recover the light of our truest Self, thus resolving our inner buried conflicts and wounds. It is thus a sign of initiation into a new path as well as the healing of the past. It is the animal equivalent of the philosopher's stone, the alchemist's tool for magical transformation where our base metal can be metamorphosized into the purest gold.

My raven is blue for she flies above the river reflecting it's color. She beckons me to follow and whispers 'trust me, for I am your soul, and any journey you take with me will be in reality a journey home - back to who you truly are.'

Extra note for 2010 revised edition:

The epilogue and final notes were both written back in late 2007 as I had plunged into a white rapid river of excitement and magic. Now, three years later, I can look back with some perspective and see how synchronistic a journey it has been. Though painful and intense, the magic has always been there, gently pulsing away under the surface, carrying me as if like an unseen blanket of divine spirit.

I still do not know where it leads, though, more recently I have been able to plug back into my dear old family within the church as well as continuing to build relationships with those of the earth-based paths.

Perhaps my future role is one of being a bridge-person – someone who knows the terrain of two different worlds and who can move between them with integrity and love. Not a proselytizer of either but a servant of both. Perhaps I am to re-claim my priesthood as a gift to be used not locked away, a priest on the margins, a priest at the edge – a hedgepriest.

And so the journey continues...

Mark at his 'place of inspiration.' The Reading
Chair in his local forest.

BOOKS

MySpiritRadio